KEEP OUT

Fleur Beale
illustrated by Marjorie Scott

Learning Media

CHAPTER 1

I've got this thing about being brave. If there's something I shouldn't do, I think, "Oh, OK, I'm not allowed to do that." And then another part of my head starts up and says, "What are you, Bruno, a scaredy cat?" So I go and do whatever it was I knew I shouldn't.

I get into so much trouble, especially from my dad. He yells at me. My heart thumps away like a pile driver, and I think, "*I only did it to be brave.*" I tell you, the inside of my head is a mess.

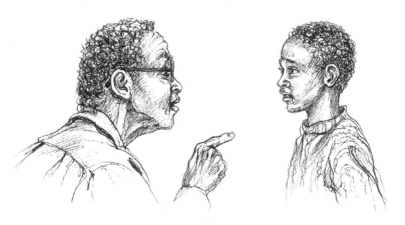

So when I saw this fence with huge signs on it saying **KEEP OUT** and in tiny letters at the bottom Our Dog Buries What It Can't Eat, well, of course, I just had to find a way in. And I did, and here I was, up in a tree with my best buddy, Eduardo. "See," I said. "It's going to be a new sports ground. And wouldn't it just be the best to ride around?"

Eduardo said we'd be in big trouble if anyone found out.

"They won't find out," I said. "Why should they?"

He looked at me and made a face. "Man, you have the shortest memory ever! We always get in trouble! And you always say we never will!"

We stared through the branches of the tree we were sitting in. "It would be fun," Eduardo said.

Down below us, we could see machinery, drainpipes, timber, piles of dirt, and huge signs saying **DANGER: KEEP OUT**.

"What if there's a dog?" Eduardo asked.

"There isn't," I said. "I've been up here four times now, and I've never seen a dog."

"It would be awesome to ride around there." His voice got all dreamy. I made myself stay still on the branch. I had him hooked!

"Don't know," I said, shaking my head. "You know, there might be a dog ...."

He spun around, making the branch jump like a rodeo bull. "Come off it, Bru! You've watched for a week. No dog, you said." He threw a twig at me. "Changed your mind, have you?"

"No-o-o," I said, drawing it out and making it sound like I might have. "It's just that you seem a bit ... you know ... sort of scared about getting caught, and ... "

"We get a rope," he snapped. "We ride back here with it. We pull the bikes up. Lower them down the other side. Dead simple."

"Yes!" I yelled, throwing both arms in the air. Not a good thing to do when you should be holding on with at least one of them. Eduardo caught me and tugged me back.

"You," he said, "are worse than slime."

"Yes," I said happily. "But sometimes it takes you a while to see how easy things can be."

He grunted, and I knew he was thinking about all the other things I'd talked him into. I said quickly, "Shall we do it now?"

He was down that tree in a second. That's one thing about Eduardo. When he makes up his mind, he doesn't sit around. It's all action.

CHAPTER 2

Back at my house, we had a problem because Dad was in the garage where the rope was. I didn't want to bother him – he got quite ticked off last time I went off with his rope.

"Where are you going to ride?" he asked.

"The sports ground," I said, which was quite true, only not the sports ground he thought.

It took half an hour, but in the end he went into the house. We stopped fiddling around with our bikes, grabbed the rope, and took off.

The new sports ground was about twenty minutes from where I lived.

"How did you find this place?" Eduardo asked as we biked beside the fence.

"It was the day you went to the dentist," I said. "I was just riding around. Then I saw the tree, so I climbed up it."

I heard him snort. "You went looking for it, you mean."

I looped the rope around my shoulder and stood on the fence post. Then I jumped up and grabbed the lowest branch. After that, it was easy.

But it was harder than I thought, getting the bikes up and out to where the branch stretched over the sports ground. "This had better be worth it, buddy," Eduardo grunted.

"Dirt, pipes, boards," I panted. "Course it'll be worth it!"

Then we had an argument about the rope. "We *can't* tie knots in it," I said. "How will we explain if we can't get them undone?"

"Can you climb up that skinny little rope if it hasn't got knots?" Eduardo demanded.

"No sweat!" I said.

I grabbed the rope and slid down.

"Now come up again!" Eduardo yelled.

That rope was so skinny and so slippery. My hands felt raw. "Give in?" yelled the smart voice from above me.

"All *right!*" I snarled. "But if we can't undo it, you're in deep trouble!"

"Better than getting stuck in here all night and turning into dog food," he said.

He didn't just tie knots in it, he tied footholds. The rope ended up so short it didn't quite reach the ground anymore.

Too bad.

He landed on the ground beside me. "This is just the best!" he said. "Let's go."

CHAPTER 3

Eduardo rode off in front of me. Then suddenly he stood on the brakes, and I crashed into him. "What did you do that for?" I yelled.

"Look!" he said. There were tire marks in the dirt in front of us. Four separate tracks. "There are other kids in here too," he whispered.

Kids … or workers on bikes? A brave person wouldn't worry about that. "There's plenty of room for all of us," I said.

I jumped on my bike and took off, Eduardo close behind me.

We went flying over huge piles of dirt and through some huge concrete pipes. You hardly had to duck your head at all.

"Hey, this is so slippery," I yelled as I rode over a line of narrow boards.

I'd forgotten all about the tire marks when suddenly we came belting around a pile of dirt at the end of the park, and there they were. Four boys, a bit older than us. They'd built a cool track.

"Look at that," I whispered as Eduardo stopped beside me. Their track went up one hill, along the board between the pipes, and down the other hill. They'd ridden really close to the dirt pile at the bottom so that they'd carved into it a bit.

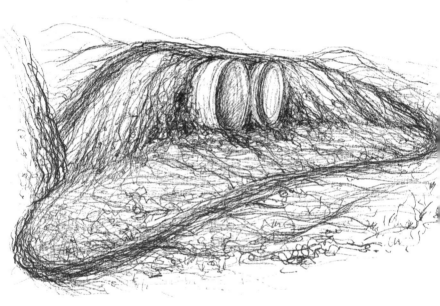

"They're good," said Eduardo. "That board must be as slippery as an eel."

"You think they'd let us have a go?" I asked. I really wanted to make that sharp turn at the bottom.

They knew we were there, but they didn't say hello or anything.

"Come on," said Eduardo. "It's more fun riding around than watching them."

We took off. "See ya!" I yelled.

They didn't answer, but I heard one of them say "How did those brats get in?"

Fine. There was plenty of room for all of us. We rode around them and kept going.

Eduardo took off and disappeared around a
bend. But a second later, he came hurtling back.
His face was pale.

"Bru! We gotta hide! There's guys in here!"

"Guys?" By the look on his face, he didn't mean
the bike guys.

"Yeah. They look mean, and they're coming
this way!" he whispered. He pushed his bike into
the nearest pipe.

"That's such a great idea!" I cried. "You might
as well paint a sign saying Eduardo Lives Here."
I pointed at the tire marks leading into the pipe.

"So what's your plan?" he snapped.

I didn't answer. I picked up my bike and threw it as far as I could to the side. Then I grabbed two lumps of wood, stood on one, and threw the other one in front of me to jump onto. "Hurry up," I called softly. "This doesn't leave tracks that show up too much. It's all I can think of."

He grunted and copied me. We threw the bikes twice more before we reached a trash heap to hide behind.

"Here they come!" Eduardo gasped, flattening himself on the dirt.

CHAPTER 4

There wasn't much room. We were squashed in between the trash heap and the side of one of the big pipes. I lay on top of my bike, not daring to move, trying not to breathe.

We heard their boots first, sucking in and out of the mud. "Look at that, will you!" The man sounded angry, but worse than that, he sounded huge. "Tire marks! How on earth are they getting bikes in here?"

Another voice grunted. "Dunno. But I'll tell you something: by the time I've finished with them, they won't be able to sit on those bikes for a week."

I prayed that they'd keep walking, but they stopped right on the other side of the heap. Their voices were loud and clear in our ears.

"When we catch them," the first guy said slowly, "I think we'll take them to the police … tell their parents and their schools." I heard his feet stamp into the ground. "This place is so darned dangerous! They have to be taught a lesson, or someone will be killed."

"We've got to find them first," said the second guy. There was silence while I held my breath for six heartbeats. "Anything there?" he called.

"Nah." The voice came from further away. "The tire marks go right through."

I could feel Eduardo shaking beside me. The man was looking in the pipe where Eduardo had wanted to hide.

"Come on," the other man called. "I've had enough of this mud. It's Sunday." I could tell he was getting angrier by the second. "Let's go and get Dave and his shepherd."

Shepherd? Why would they want a shepherd to find us? Suddenly I went cold. Did he mean a German shepherd? A huge, big dog with huge, big teeth? We had to get out of there. Thank goodness Eduardo had tied knots in the rope.

We lay there, listening to their footsteps getting fainter, and then we lay there very still for a while longer, listening to nothing at all.

It seemed like hours before Eduardo finally whispered, "Let's go. We don't want to be around when they come back."

I didn't answer. I just got on my bike and started riding as fast as I could. The tree and the rope were right on the other side of the grounds.

"Shall we tell those other guys?" Eduardo gasped as we raced by them.

"Nah! Let them fry," I said.

And that was when it happened. You know how it is when you watch TV, and everything's in slow motion? Well, that's what it was like.

The rider who'd called us brats was cutting his bike in at the bottom of the dirt heap. He put a foot down to stop himself from falling. Suddenly, the whole side of the pile just slid down. He put up his hands and tried to run, but the dirt fell on him like it had been let loose from a dump truck.

The three others stood where they were, holding their bikes, their mouths wide open. We dropped our bikes and raced over, but even before we got there, they were moving. "Let's get out of here!" one of them yelled, and they turned to run.

I couldn't believe it, and Eduardo was already scrabbling at the dirt with his bare hands.

"Stop!" I yelled at the others. "Get back here! Help us!" I started digging too, but I kept on yelling.

They didn't come back.

"Eduardo, we need help!" I gasped. There was too much dirt – we'd never do it by ourselves.

"You go!" Eduardo grunted the words out.

I jumped on my bike and rode the race of my life to get to the tree.

CHAPTER 5

How long does it take for someone to die? I didn't know. I got to the tree and was up the rope in seconds. I jumped down on the other side and pushed through the bushes. I saw the main road. What now? I ran to the side of the road and waved my arms around. "Help! Help!" I screamed as cars raced by.

"Stop! Somebody stop!" I was counting down the seconds that Brat-boy had left to live.

Suddenly, there was an ambulance, right there in front of me! An ambulance had stopped. I couldn't believe it. "What's the matter, son?" the driver called, leaning out her window.

"Over there!" I said. "In the park. There's a landslide! A kid's buried!"

"Show me," the driver said as she grabbed a shovel. The paramedic beside her jumped out. "Bring the gear," the driver called. "Follow us."

We ran. They left the ambulance where it had stopped by the side of the road.

"That's the tree," I gasped.

She threw the shovel over the fence, and in seconds, she'd jumped from the post to the branch and had swung up into the tree. Behind me, I could hear the man crashing through the bushes. He pushed in front of me.

"Bring this," he said, shoving a black bag at me, and then he too was above me and swinging up into the leaves.

"Go to your left!" I yelled. "Follow the fence!"

I still don't know how I got the bag up the tree. I just remember I was suddenly on the ground running. One of the paramedics must have ridden off on my bike because it was gone.

How much time had been used up? Time goes so quickly when there isn't enough of it. When I got there, everyone was digging. The man had the shovel, and the woman used her bare hands. Eduardo was still digging, but more slowly.

I threw myself down beside them and used my bare hands too. Seconds later, we uncovered his feet …. Then we had his legs out.

"Just a bit more," gasped the man. "OK. We should be able to pull him out now." He kept shoveling at the dirt, but the three of us grabbed the boy's legs and pulled.

He came free. I wanted to cheer, but the words died in my throat when I saw his face. It was *blue*.

CHAPTER 6

"**I**s he dead?" I gasped the words, but nobody answered. Eduardo flopped onto the ground beside me, panting for breath. His hands were bleeding. The woman had her fingers on the boy's neck.

"We've got a pulse, but it's weak," she said.

The man had the bag open. He put a tube or something in Brat-boy's mouth. Then he put a mask with a bag on it over the boy's mouth and nose. He pumped the bag in and out. The woman reached over. "I'd better do that. My hands are too cut up to do anything else."

I watched their faces, looking for a flicker to show that they were winning, that Brat-boy would live. The man put a collar thing round the boy's neck. Then he checked him carefully all over.

I heard footsteps running from the direction of the tree. It was a policeman. The woman looked up without stopping the pumping.

"Get the ambulance in here. We need the oxygen."

The policeman spoke into his radio. "It's on its way," he said. "They've just got to get the gates open." He ran toward the gate, still talking into his radio. I kept my eyes on Brat-boy. "Live! Live!" I screamed in my head.

Seconds later, the ambulance was there, another police officer at the wheel. The paramedics connected Brat-boy up to the oxygen. They were strapping him onto a stretcher when Eduardo asked, "Is he going to live?"

The woman glanced up and smiled at us. "He's got a good chance. I think we got him out in time, thanks to you two."

Eduardo and I looked at each other and smiled. We were heroes!

One of the police officers came over to us. "What's his name?" he asked.

We stared at him. "We don't know," I said. "He wasn't with us."

"His friends took off when it happened," Eduardo added.

"Hmm," said the cop. He moved off, following the ambulance and talking into his radio.

"Let's get out of here," I muttered to Eduardo, but it was too late. Running toward us were three men. One of them was being pulled along by a dog that looked as big as an elephant.

"What's going on?" the biggest man roared. "Police! Ambulance! Will *somebody* tell me what's happening here?"

CHAPTER 7

Eduardo and I looked at the dog. It was pulling hard at its lead. The man holding it gave a command, and the dog sat at his feet, quiet and still. Like Brat-boy.

"Start talking," said the big man. He stood over us, huge and threatening.

"Back at the station, I think," said the police officer.

They bundled us into a car, throwing our bikes in the trunk. We didn't say anything for the whole ride. They really let us have it once we got to the station. Those park guys were mad enough to feed us to their dog. They fired questions at us:

"How did you get in?"

"How often have you been there?"

We told them about the tree. The big guy grabbed a telephone without even asking if he could use it. "Ben? Get a chain saw and take off the branch of that walnut. You know, the one that hangs over the fence."

At first I was sorry, but then I was glad. I knew I'd never be brave enough to go back there. The park man said one more thing before he put the phone down. "And, Ben, cut up that rope while you're at it."

Great! Dad was not going to be pleased about any of this. The big man slammed the phone down and glared at us. I was not feeling brave at all. I'd have given just about anything to be able to run out of there and never see him again. I hated him, and I hated myself.

"Didn't you see the signs. Can't you read?" he yelled. "Well?" he demanded when we didn't answer.

I guess Eduardo's braver than me. "Yes," he said, "we can read."

"So you came in anyway!" the man shouted. "How are you going to feel if your friend dies? Eh? Tell me that!"

"He's not our friend," I muttered, my eyes on the floor.

There was a sudden silence. "You mean you don't like him anymore?" the dog man asked.

I shook my head. "No. I mean we don't know who he is."

"His friends ran away when the dirt fell on him," Eduardo added. "There were three of them."

I managed to glance up. All three men were staring at us, and you could almost see the thoughts whirling round in their heads.

"You mean there were *two* lots of you in there?" demanded the dog man.

We nodded.

The big man let loose a string of words that made even the cop raise his eyebrows. "Do you know how they got in?" he barked.

We shook our heads. He grabbed the phone again. After he'd told Ben with the chain saw the whole story, he growled, "Phone your parents. I want to talk to them."

We looked at the officer. Maybe he'd save us. Some hope.

"Good idea," the officer said.

I tried being polite. "You can ring first," I said to Eduardo.

He shook his head. "Mom and Dad won't be home yet. They went to some wedding."

I picked up the phone and tried to think about all the brave people I'd ever heard of. I won't tell you about that phone call. I'll just say that it isn't the greatest buzz in the world to phone your dad and ask him to come and get you from the police station.

CHAPTER 8

"I hope he belts your backside so hard you can't sit down for a week," snarled the big park man.

Suddenly I'd had enough. I felt something snap in my head. I jumped up. "Listen!" I yelled. "I know we were stupid! I know we shouldn't have been there! But if Eduardo and I hadn't been there, then that kid would be dead. People would say it was your fault. They'd say you should've had better security. You knew that tree was there! And what about those other kids? How did they get in?" I added.

Before they could yell at me, Dad came in. He wasn't wearing his usual grin.

He didn't say much on the way home, but that night he went out to the garage and removed the front wheel of my bike. "You can have it back in three months," was all he said. Oh, except for the bit where he said I could earn a new rope by cleaning the car every weekend for six weeks, mowing the lawn for the next three, and cooking dinner every Wednesday from now until I lost all my teeth and hair.

"There's only one good thing about what you did," he finished up.

"Oh, you mean saving a kid's life?" I asked.

He ignored that. "You kept your head in an emergency. You get full marks for that. You did a good job." He looked at me over his glasses. "If you are going to be the kind of kid who's always looking for excitement, and it seems that you are, then it's just as well you've got a good head on you."

"Gee, thanks, Dad." I wished I could tell him about the brave thing. But when I tried, the words wouldn't come. I was a wimp, and I wanted to hide under a stone.

There was a huge fuss about the whole thing, but Dad wouldn't let the reporters talk to me. I kept looking for photographers on motorbikes. I thought they'd sneak up on me and take my photograph when I wasn't looking.

It didn't happen.

People talked more about the three boys who ran away than they did about us. You should have heard the talk-back radio. It made me sick listening to all that. I mean, you don't know what you'll do in an emergency. How do those people know they wouldn't take off and leave a friend under the dirt?

A few days later, the phone went, and Dad told the reporter no, she couldn't talk to me. He put the phone down. Then he put an arm round my shoulders. "Have I told you I'm so proud of you I could burst?"

I stared at him. "Are you?"

He gave me a funny sort of smile. "Of course. What you and Eduardo did took guts. You thought of someone else, not yourselves." He gave me a hug.

About two weeks after that, I suddenly realized that the brave thing had faded away. I even told Dad about it because I was kind of surprised. He looked thoughtful. "So why do you reckon it doesn't bug you now?" he asked.

"I think," I said slowly, "that even if that kid had died, Eduardo and I would still know we'd done our best. We really tried. It wasn't anything about being brave." I stopped. I couldn't explain.

Dad ruffled my hair and looked happy, so I tried asking for my front wheel back.

"No dice," he said, "but how about I take you and Eduardo surfing? I think you'd like that."

He was right. We do. Life's a buzz!